HEBREW ALPHABET
Coloring Book

Chaya Burstein

DOVER PUBLICATIONS, INC., NEW YORK

Special thanks to Robert Hoberman
for checking the Hebrew material.

Copyright © 1986 by Chaya Burstein.

Published in Canada by General Publishing Company, Ltd., 30 Lesmill Road, Don Mills, Toronto, Ontario.
Published in the United Kingdom by Constable and Company, Ltd.

Hebrew Alphabet Coloring Book is a new work, first published by Dover Publications, Inc., in 1986.

International Standard Book Number: 0-486-25089-X

Manufactured in the United States of America
Dover Publications, Inc., 31 East 2nd Street, Mineola, N.Y. 11501

PREFACE

This book will help you learn the twenty-two letters of the Hebrew alphabet and over 250 Modern Hebrew words while you color. Each Hebrew letter has its own page containing common Hebrew words beginning with that letter. Near each word is a picture of the thing it stands for. When you color a picture, see if you can read its name in Hebrew.

You can see that each Hebrew word has a small number next to it. To find out what a Hebrew word means, just check the bottom of the page for the English word with the same number. There is also a "Vocabulary" section in the back of the book. You can use this section to look up a word in English and find out what it is in Hebrew.

Hebrew is read from right to left, and a true Hebrew book opens from right to left: it starts at what we would call the "back" and ends at what we would call the "front." To give you an idea of what this looks like, the back of this book shows an alphabet the way it would look in a real Hebrew book: it starts on page 32 and ends on page 30.

HOW HEBREW IS PRONOUNCED

There are two chief ways in which Hebrew can be pronounced. One way is called "Ashkenazic" (Germanic). It has been used in Europe for many years. The other way is called "Sephardic" (Spanish). It is used in Israel and the Middle East. In this book, the explanation of pronunciation follows the Sephardic way.

The Alphabet

א   sounds like a slight catch in the throat, like the one between the two syllables of "uh-uh," or else it is silent

ב   sounds like the b in "bed"

ג   sounds like the g in "go"

ד   sounds like the d in "dog"

ה   sounds like the h in "hat" (it is silent at the end of a word)

ו   sounds like the v in "vote" (it can also stand for vowels; see the section on vowel signs)

ז   sounds like the z in "zoo"

ח   sounds like the rough h at the beginning of "Hanukkah"

ט   sounds like the t in "toy"

י   sounds like the y in "yes" (it can also stand for a vowel; see the section on vowel signs)

כ   sounds like the k in "king"

ל   sounds like the l in "like"

מ   sounds like the m in "milk"

נ   sounds like the n in "no"

ס   sounds like the s in "sing"

ע   sounds like a slight catch in the throat, like the one between the two syllables of "uh-uh," or else it is silent

פ   sounds like the p in "pet"

צ   sounds like the ts at the end of "cats"

ק sounds like the k in "king"

ר sounds like the r in "ring"

שׁ sounds like the sh in "shoe"

ת sounds like the t in "toy"

For certain letters, the sound changes when a dot is taken away or moved:

בּ sounds like the b in "bed," but ב sounds like the v in "vote"

כּ sounds like the k in "king," but כ sounds like the rough h at the beginning of "Hanukkah"

פּ sounds like the p in "pet," but פ sounds like the f in "father"

שׁ sounds like the sh in "shoe," but שׂ sounds like the s in "sing"

In this book, the letter *tav* also has a dot whenever it appears at the beginning of a word (and sometimes in the middle of a word). Although in Sephardic Hebrew, *tav*—with or without a dot—sounds like the t in "toy," in Ashkenazic Hebrew *tav* with a dot sounds like the t in "toy," but without a dot sounds like the s in "sing."

Hebrew prayer books will also show a dot in other letters, especially *gimmel* and *dalet*. This book does not show a dot in any of these letters, because each letter now sounds the same—with or without a dot—for all Hebrew speakers.

A small mark to the upper left of a letter can also change the sound:

ג sounds like the g in "go," but ג׳ sounds like the j in "jump"

Final Letters

There are five letters in the Hebrew alphabet that look different when they are at the end of a word. The final forms are included in the running alphabet at the end of the book.

כ becomes	ך	פ becomes	ף
מ becomes	ם	צ becomes	ץ
נ becomes	ן		

Vowel Signs

Classical Hebrew, the language of the Bible, was written without showing vowels. Many years later a system of vowel signs was developed. Vowels are not usually shown in Modern Hebrew writing except in books for beginning readers. Here are the vowel signs you will find in this book:

Some vowel signs are written under the letter.

VOWEL SIGN	PRONUNCIATION
ָ	a as in "father," but cut short
ַ	a as in "father," but cut short
ֲ	a as in "father," but cut short
ֵ	e as in "they," but cut short
ֶ	e as in "met"
ִ	ee as in "feet"
ֻ	oo as in "too"
ְ	silent most of the time; sometimes a short uh sound as in "uh-huh"

Other vowel signs are joined with a letter.

VOWEL SIGN	PRONUNCIATION
יִ	ee as in "feet" (the dot is written under the letter before the י)
וֹ	o as in "more," but cut short
וּ	oo as in "too"

Stress

When you listen to a Hebrew word, you will notice that some syllables sound "stronger" than others. These strong syllables are called "stressed" (or "accented") syllables. In Hebrew, it is usually the last syllable of a word that is stressed.

ALEPH

1: Airplane. 2: Goose. 3: Tree. 4: Pine tree. 5: Father. 6: Mother. 7: Brother. 8: Sister. 9: Bicycle. 10: Pear. 11: Watermelon. 12: Food. 13: Finger. 14: Stag. 15: Tent. 16: Lion.

5

בֹּקֶר ¹

בֶּדְוִי ²

בֵּן ³

בַּנַּאי ¹⁵

בַּיִת ¹⁴

בֹּטְנִים ¹³

בַּר-מִצְוָה ⁵

בַּת-מִצְוָה ⁶

בְּהֵמוֹת ¹¹

בֶּטֶן ¹²

בְּרְוָז ⁴

בִּימָה ⁷

בָּשָׂר ¹⁰

בֵּיצִים ⁸

בָּצָל ⁹

BET

1: Morning. 2: Bedouin. 3: Son. 4: Duck. 5: Bar Mitzvah. 6: Bat Mitzvah. 7: Stage, pulpit. 8: Eggs. 9: Onion. 10: Meat. 11: Behemoth (large beast). 12: Belly. 13: Peanuts. 14: House. 15: Builder.

ג׳ירָפָה¹

גָּדֵר²

גָּן³

גַּנָּב⁴

גֶּדֶר⁵

גָּדֵר⁶

גַּלְגִּלִית⁷

גְלִידָה⁸

גִּבּוֹר⁹

גָּמָל¹⁰

גּוּר¹¹

גֶּשֶׁם¹²

GIMMEL

1: Giraffe. 2: Carrots. 3: Garden. 4: Thief. 5: Kid.
6: Fence. 7: Roller skate. 8: Ice cream. 9: Strong man.
10: Camel. 11: Cub. 12: Rain.

דְּבוֹרָה 13

דֶּגֶל 12

דֶּקֶל 1

דּוֹדָה 10

דֶּלֶת 11

דּוֹד 9

דָּב 4

דַּוָּר 8

דֶּרֶך 7

דָּג 5

דְּבוֹן 3

דְּבַשׁ 2

דָּג 6

DALET

1: Palm tree. 2: Honey. 3: Bear cub. 4: Bear. 5: Fisherman. 6: Fish. 7: Road. 8: Mailman. 9: Uncle. 10: Aunt. 11: Door. 12: Flag. 13: Bee.

הַר גַּעַשׁ [8]

הֵיכָל [7]

הַרְפַּתְקָה [1]

הִתְאַהֵב [2]

הָמוֹן [3]

הֹדִּי [6]

הוֹרָה [5]

הוֹרִים [4]

HEY

1: Adventure. 2: Fell in love. 3: Crowd. 4: Parents.
5: Hora (dance). 6: Indian. 7: Temple. 8: Volcano.

VAV

1: House. 2: Curtains. 3: Committee. 4: Argument.
5: Wadi (ravine, riverbed). 6: Waltz. 7: Rose.

ZAYIN

1: Old man. 2: Beard. 3: Glutton. 4: Gold. 5: Glass. 6: Crawler, reptile. 7: Manure, rubbish. 8: Flies. 9: Song. 10: Singer (male). 11: Singer (female). 12: Nightingale. 13: Wolves. 14: Pair. 15: Comet.

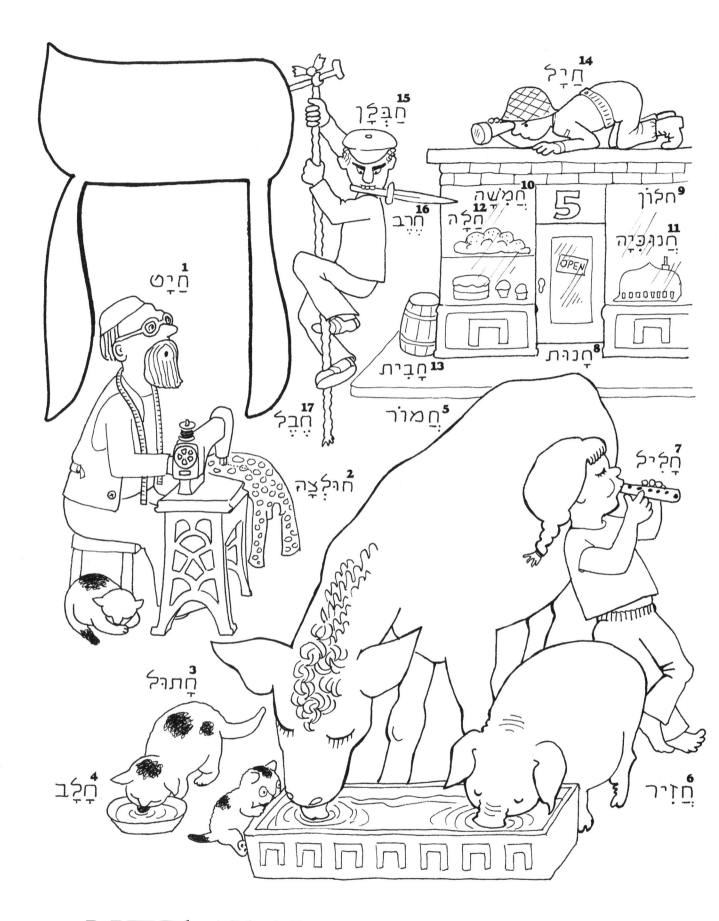

HET

1: Tailor. 2: Shirt. 3: Cat. 4: Milk. 5: Donkey. 6: Pig. 7: Recorder, flute. 8: Store. 9: Window. 10: Five. 11: Hanukkah lamp. 12: Hallah (Sabbath bread). 13: Barrel. 14: Soldier. 15: Saboteur. 16: Sword. 17: Rope.

טַיָס ⁵

טִיּוּל ⁶

טַבָּח ⁴

טֶלֶפוֹן ³

טְרַקְטוֹר ²

טֶנִיס ¹

TET

1: Tennis. 2: Tractor. 3: Telephone.
4: Cook. 5: Pilot. 6: Hike.

YOD

1: Ostrich. 2: Ibex. 3: Vegetables. 4: Pigeon. 5: Wine.
6: Girl. 7: Barefoot (female). 8: Birthday. 9: Forest.
10: Moon.

כּוֹכָב 13
כַּלָּה 10
כְּפִיר 9
כְּפִיר 12
כִּנּוֹר 11
כֹּתֶל 8
כֶּרֶם 1
כּוֹבַע 2
כִּסֵּא 7
כַּדוּרֶגֶל 3
כַּדּוּר 4
כֶּבֶשׂ 6
כֶּלֶב 5

KAF

1: Vineyard. 2: Hat. 3: Soccer. 4: Ball. 5: Dog. 6: Lamb.
7: Chair. 8: Wall. 9: Young lion. 10: Bride. 11: Violin.
12: "Kfir" jet. 13: Star.

לִימוֹן **7**

לֵיצָן **6**

לָמַד **1**

לְבִיבוֹת **2**

לֵב **5**

לֶחֶם **3**

לוּל **4**

LAMED

1: Scholar. 2: Pancakes. 3: Bread. 4: Chicken coop.
5: Heart. 6: Clown. 7: Lemon.

MEM

1: Teacher (female). 2: Eyeglasses. 3: Fortress. 4: Tower. 5: Star of David. 6: Helicopter.
7: Airplane. 8: Umbrella. 9: King. 10: Queen. 11: Melon. 12: Cucumber. 13: Juice.
14: Flood. 15: Taxi. 16: Letter. 17: Suitcase. 18: Hundred. 19: Matzah.

NUN

1: Woodpecker. 2: Snake. 3: Tiger. 4: Buds, sprouts.
5: Grandchild. 6: Prophet. 7: Paper. 8: Speech.
9: Girls. 10: Swing. 11: Candle.

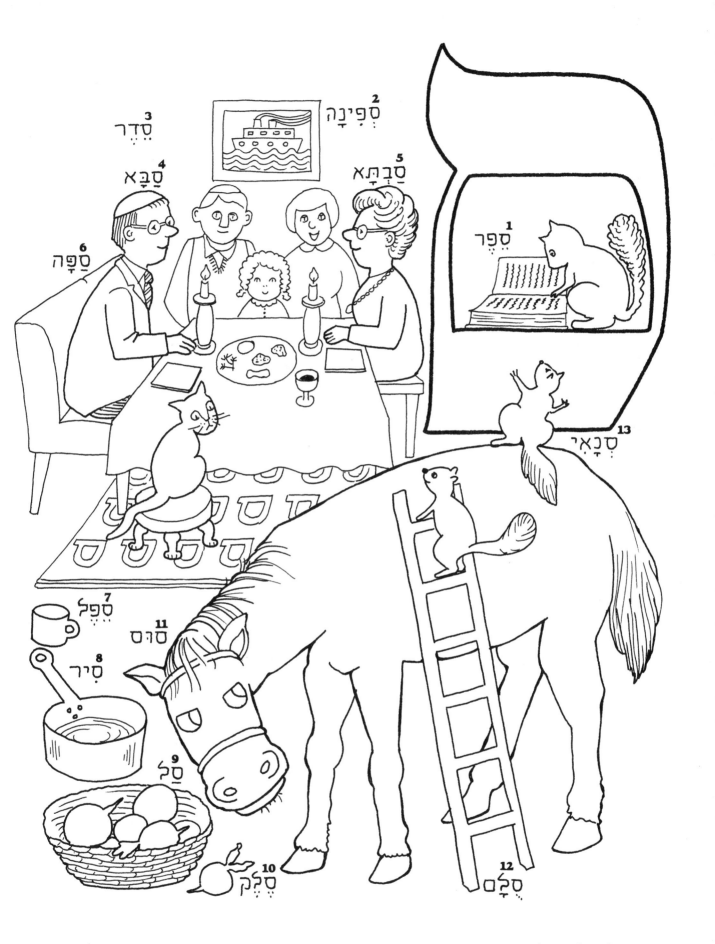

SAMEH

1: Book. 2: Ship. 3: Seder (Passover meal). 4: Grandfather. 5: Grandmother. 6: Couch. 7: Cup. 8: Pot. 9: Basket. 10: Beet. 11: Horse. 12: Ladder. 13: Squirrel.

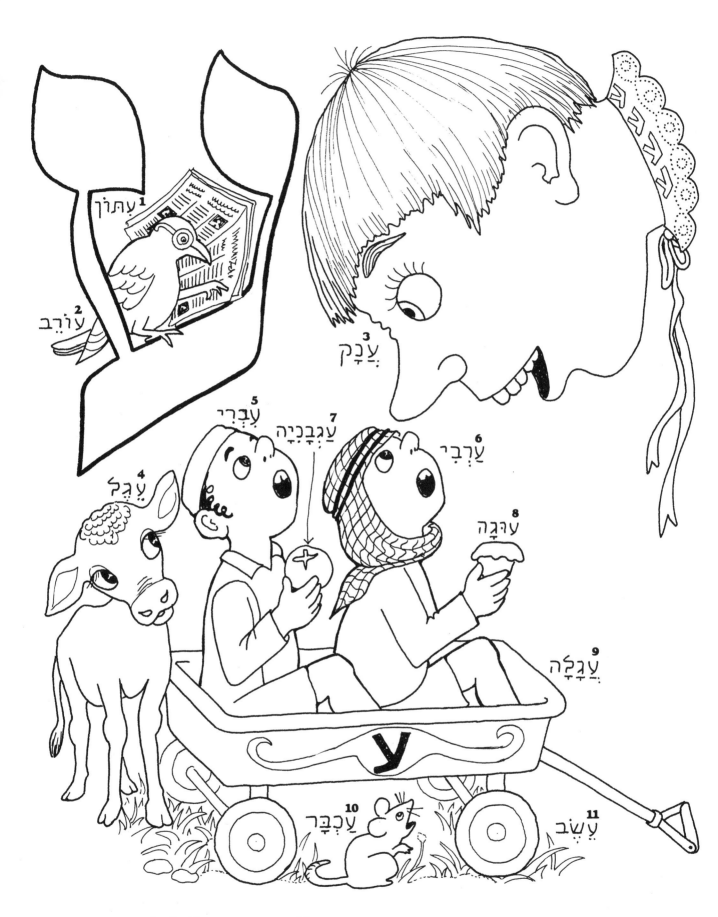

AYIN

1: Newspaper. 2: Crow. 3: Giant. 4: Calf. 5: Hebrew
(Jew). 6: Arab. 7: Tomato. 8: Cake. 9: Wagon.
10: Mouse. 11: Grass.

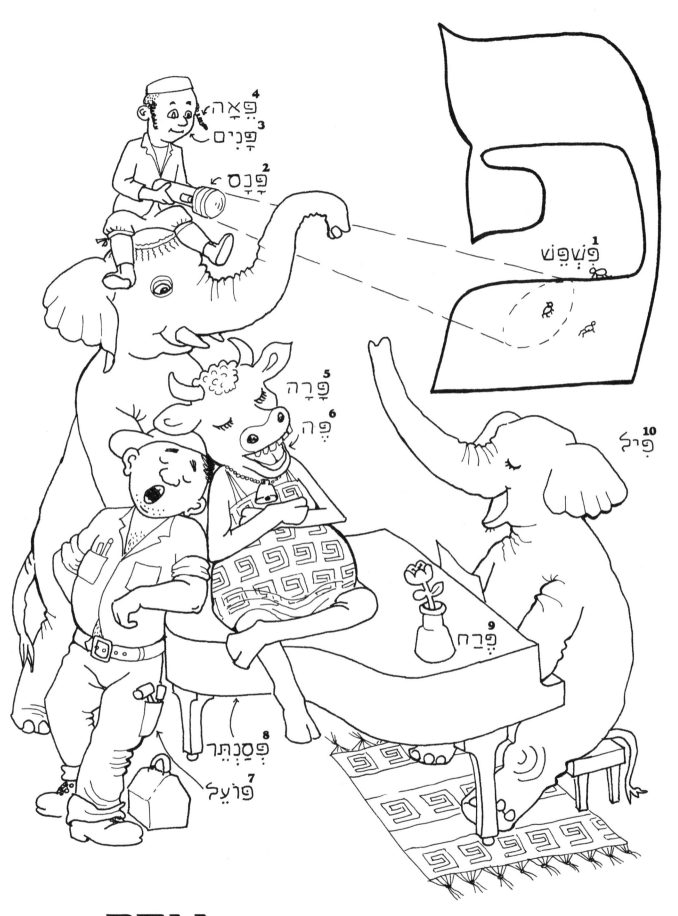

PEH

1: Bug. 2: Flashlight. 3: Face. 4: Earlock. 5: Cow.
6: Mouth. 7: Worker. 8: Piano. 9: Flower. 10: Elephant.

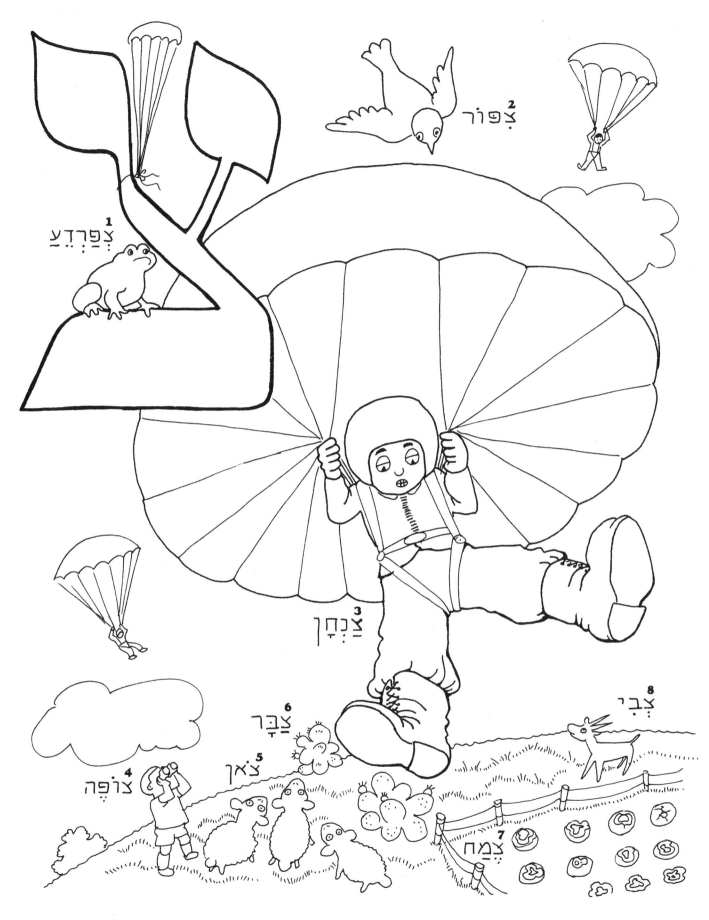

TZADI

1: Frog. 2: Bird. 3: Parachutist. 4: Scout. 5: Sheep and goats. 6: Cactus, prickly pear. 7: Plant. 8: Deer, gazelle.

KOF

1: Monkey. 2: Peel. 3: Magician. 4: Coffee. 5: Teakettle.
6: Nest. 7: Contractor. 8: Kangaroo. 9: Porcupine.
10: Rhinoceros. 11: Straw.

רַכֶּבֶת 2

רַקְדָנִית 3

רִבָּה 10

JAM

ALEF BET STREET

רְחוֹב 9

רַכֶּפֶת 1

רוֹפְאָה 8

רַב 4

רַגְלַיִם 6

ר ר ר ר ר ר

רֹאשׁ 5

רִצְפָּה 7

RESH

1: Cyclamen. 2: Train. 3: Dancer (female). 4: Rabbi.
5: Head. 6: Feet. 7: Floor. 8: Doctor (female). 9: Street.
10: Jam.

שָׁמַיִם ²

שֵׁד ³

שָׁעוֹן ⁴

שׁוּעָל ¹

שׁוּק ⁵

שׁוֹטֵר ¹⁴

שׁוּם ⁹

שֵׂעָר ¹³

שְׂמַרְטַף ¹²

שָׂפָם ¹⁵

שְׁמוֹנָה ⁸

שִׁשָּׁה ⁶

שֶׂה ¹⁶

שָׁפָן ¹⁷

שִׁבְעָה ⁷

שְׁלִישִׁיָּה ¹⁰

שְׂמִיכָה ¹¹

SHIN/SIN

1: Fox. 2: Sky. 3: Demon. 4: Watch. 5: Market. 6: Six. 7: Seven.
8: Eight. 9: Garlic. 10: Triplet. 11: Blanket. 12: Baby-sitter. 13: Hair.
14: Policeman. 15: Mustache. 16: Lamb. 17: Rabbit.

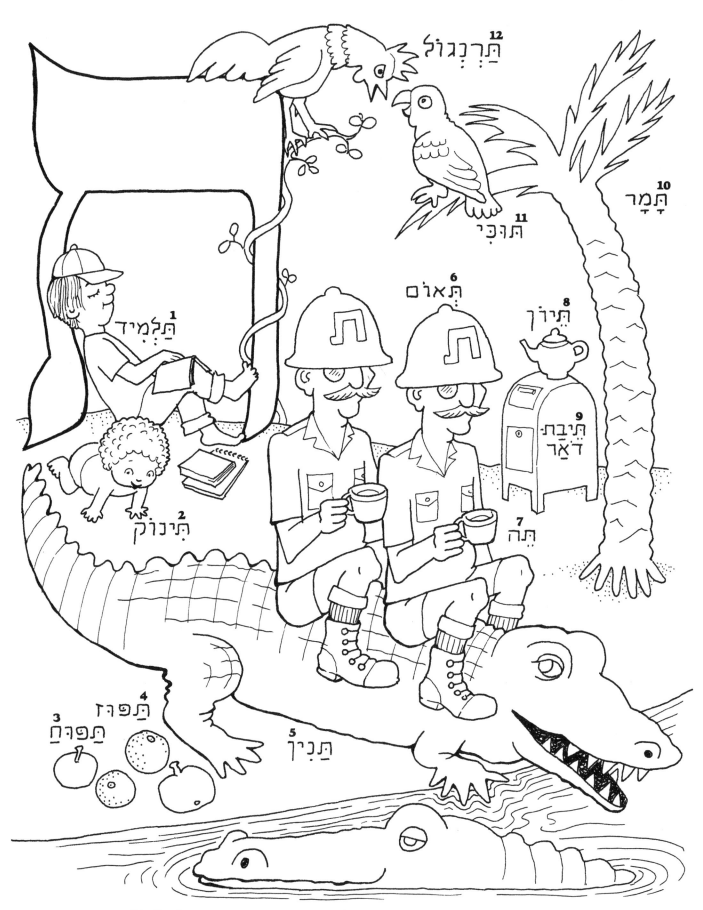

12 תַּרְנְגוֹל

11 תֻּכִּי

10 תָּמָר

6 תְּאוֹם

8 תֵּיוֹן

1 תַּלְמִיד

9 תֵּיבַת דֹּאַר

2 תִּינוֹק

7 תֵּה

4 תַּפּוּז

3 תַּפּוּחַ

5 תַּנִּין

TAV

1: Pupil. 2: Baby. 3: Apple. 4: Orange. 5: Crocodile.
6: Twin. 7: Tea. 8: Teapot. 9: Mailbox. 10: Date palm.
11: Parrot. 12: Rooster.

VOCABULARY

adventure	הַרְפַּתְקָה	cactus	צָבָר	door	דֶּלֶת
airplane	אֲוִירוֹן, מָטוֹס	cake	עוּגָה	duck	בַּרְוָז
apple	תַּפּוּחַ	calf	עֵגֶל		
Arab	עֲרָבִי	camel	גָּמָל		
argument	וִכּוּחַ	candle	נֵר	earlock	פֵּאָה
aunt	דּוֹדָה	carrots	גֶּזֶר	eggs	בֵּיצִים
		cat	חָתוּל	eight	שְׁמוֹנָה
		chair	כִּסֵּא	elephant	פִּיל
baby	תִּינוֹק	chicken coop	לוּל	eyeglasses	מִשְׁקָפַיִם
baby-sitter	שְׁמַרְטַף	clown	לֵיצָן		
ball	כַּדּוּר	coffee	קָפֶה		
barefoot (female)	יְחֵפָה	comet	זִיק	face	פָּנִים
Bar Mitzvah	בַּר־מִצְוָה	committee	וַעַד	father	אַבָּא
barrel	חָבִית	contractor	קַבְּלָן	feet	רַגְלַיִם
basket	סַל	cook	טַבָּח	fell in love	הִתְאַהֵב
Bat Mitzvah	בַּת־מִצְוָה	couch	סַפָּה	fence	גָּדֵר
bear	דֹּב	cow	פָּרָה	finger	אֶצְבַּע
bear cub	דֻּבּוֹן	crawler	זוֹחֵל	fish	דָּג
beard	זָקָן	crocodile	תַּנִּין	fisherman	דַּיָּג
Bedouin	בֶּדְוִי	crow	עוֹרֵב	five	חֲמִשָּׁה
bee	דְּבוֹרָה	crowd	הָמוֹן	flag	דֶּגֶל
beet	סֶלֶק	cub	גּוּר	flashlight	פָּנָס
behemoth	בְּהֵמוֹת	cucumber	מְלָפְפוֹן	flies	זְבוּבִים
belly	בֶּטֶן	cup	סֵפֶל	flood	מַבּוּל
bicycle	אוֹפַנַּיִם	curtains	וִילוֹנוֹת	floor	רִצְפָּה
bird	צִפּוֹר	cyclamen	רַקֶּפֶת	flower	פֶּרַח
birthday	יוֹם הוּלֶדֶת			flute	חָלִיל
blanket	שְׂמִיכָה			food	אֹכֶל
book	סֵפֶר	dancer (female)	רַקְדָנִית	forest	יַעַר
bread	לֶחֶם	date palm	תָּמָר	fortress	מִבְצָר
bride	כַּלָּה	deer	צְבִי	fox	שׁוּעָל
brother	אָח	demon	שֵׁד	frog	צְפַרְדֵּעַ
buds	נִצָּנִים	doctor (female)	רוֹפְאָה		
bug	פִּשְׁפֵּשׁ	dog	כֶּלֶב		
builder	בַּנַּאי	donkey	חֲמוֹר	garden	גַּן

English	Hebrew	English	Hebrew	English	Hebrew
garlic	שׁוּם	"Kfir" jet	כְּפִיר	palm tree	דֶּקֶל
gazelle	צְבִי	kid (goat)	גְּדִי	pancakes	לְבִיבוֹת
giant	עֲנָק	king	מֶלֶךְ	paper	נְיָר
giraffe	ג׳יֽרָפָה			parachutist	צַנְחָן
girl	יַלְדָּה			parents	הוֹרִים
girls	נְעָרוֹת	ladder	סֻלָּם	parrot	תֻּכִּי
glass	זְכוּכִית	lamb	כֶּבֶשׂ, שֶׂה	peanuts	בֹּטְנִים
glutton	זוֹלֵל	lemon	לִימוֹן	pear	אַגָּס
gold	זָהָב	letter	מִכְתָּב	peel	קְלִיפָּה
goose	אַוָּז	lion	אֲרִי	piano	פְּסַנְתֵּר
grandchild	נֶכֶד	lion, young	כְּפִיר	pig	חֲזִיר
grandfather	סַבָּא			pigeon	יוֹנָה
grandmother	סַבְתָּא			pilot	טַיָּס
grass	עֵשֶׂב	magician	קוֹסֵם	pine tree	אֹרֶן
		mailbox	תֵּיבַת־דֹּאַר	plant	צֶמַח
		mailman	דַּוָּר	policeman	שׁוֹטֵר
hair	שֵׂעָר	manure	זֶבֶל	porcupine	קִפּוֹד
hallah	חַלָּה	market	שׁוּק	pot	סִיר
Hanukkah lamp	חֲנוּכִּיָּה	matzah	מַצָּה	prickly pear	צַבָּר
hat	כּוֹבַע	meat	בָּשָׂר	prophet	נָבִיא
head	רֹאשׁ	melon	מֶלוֹן	pulpit	בִּימָה
heart	לֵב	milk	חָלָב	pupil	תַּלְמִיד
Hebrew (Jew)	עִבְרִי	monkey	קוֹף		
helicopter	מָסוֹק	moon	יָרֵחַ		
hike	טִיּוּל	morning	בֹּקֶר	queen	מַלְכָּה
honey	דְּבַשׁ	mother	אִמָּא		
hora	הוֹרָה	mouse	עַכְבָּר		
horse	סוּס	mouth	פֶּה	rabbi	רַב
house	בַּיִת, וִילָה	mustache	שָׂפָם	rabbit	שָׁפָן
hundred	מֵאָה			rain	גֶּשֶׁם
				recorder	חָלִיל
		nest	קֵן	reptile	זוֹחֵל
ibex	יָעֵל	newspaper	עִתּוֹן	rhinoceros	קַרְנַף
ice cream	גְּלִידָה	nightingale	זָמִיר	road	דֶּרֶךְ
Indian	הֹדִי			roller skate	גַּלְגִּילִית
				rooster	תַּרְנְגוֹל
		old man	זָקֵן	rope	חֶבֶל
jam	רִבָּה	onion	בָּצָל	rose	וֶרֶד
Jew	עִבְרִי	orange	תַּפּוּז	rubbish	זֶבֶל
juice	מִיץ	ostrich	יָעֵן		
				saboteur	חַבְּלָן
kangaroo	קֶנְגּוּרוּ	pair	זוּג	scholar	לַמְדָן

scout	צוֹפֶה	street	רְחוֹב	twin	תְּאוֹם
Seder	סֵדֶר	strong man	גִּבּוֹר		
seven	שִׁבְעָה	suitcase	מִזְוָדָה		
sheep and goats	צֹאן	swing	נַדְנֵדָה	umbrella	מִטְרִיָּה
ship	סְפִינָה	sword	חֶרֶב	uncle	דּוֹד
shirt	חוּלְצָה				
singer (female)	זַמֶּרֶת				
singer (male)	זַמָּר	tailor	חַיָּט	vegetables	יְרָקוֹת
sister	אָחוֹת	taxi	מוֹנִית	vineyard	כֶּרֶם
six	שִׁשָּׁה	tea	תֵּה	violin	כִּנּוֹר
sky	שָׁמַיִם	teacher (female)	מוֹרָה	volcano	הַר גַּעַשׁ
snake	נָחָשׁ	teakettle	קוּמְקוּם		
soccer	כַּדּוּרֶגֶל	teapot	תֵּיּוֹן		
soldier	חַיָּל	telephone	טֶלֶפוֹן	wadi	וָדִי
son	בֵּן	temple	הֵיכָל	wagon	עֲגָלָה
song	זְמִירָה	tennis	טֶנִיס	wall	כֹּתֶל
speech	נְאוּם	tent	אֹהֶל	waltz	וַלְס
sprouts	נִצָּנִים	thief	גַּנָּב	watch	שָׁעוֹן
squirrel	סְנָאִי	tiger	נָמֵר	watermelon	אֲבַטִּיחַ
stag	אַיָּל	tomato	עַגְבָנִיָּה	window	חַלּוֹן
stage	בִּימָה	tower	מִגְדָּל	wine	יַיִן
star	כּוֹכָב	tractor	טְרַקְטוֹר	wolves	זְאֵבִים
Star of David	מָגֵן דָּוִד	train	רַכֶּבֶת	woodpecker	נַקָּר
store	חֲנוּת	tree	אִילָן	worker	פּוֹעֵל
straw	קַשׁ	triplet	שְׁלִישִׁיָּה		

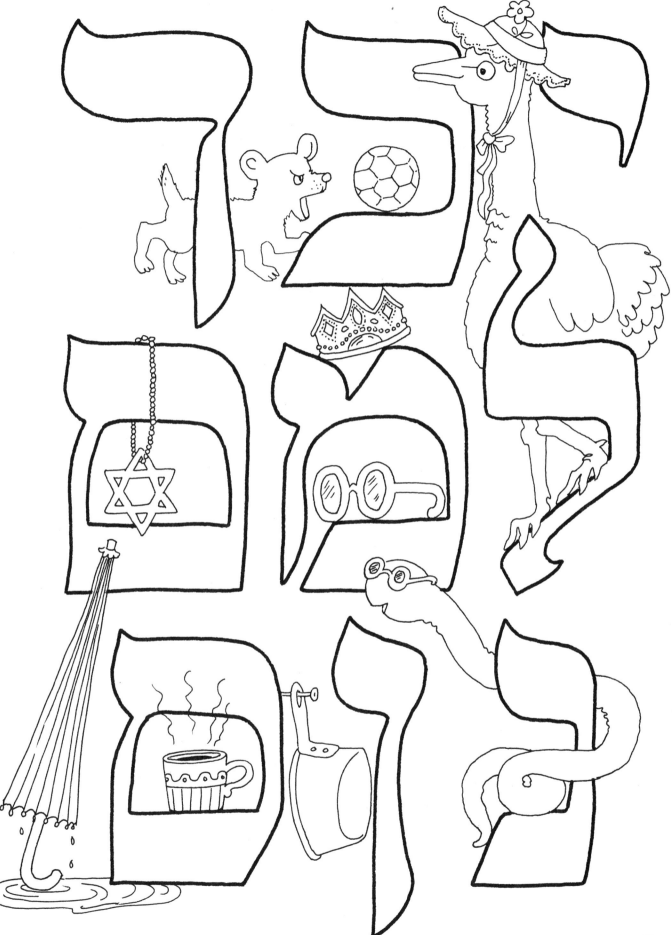

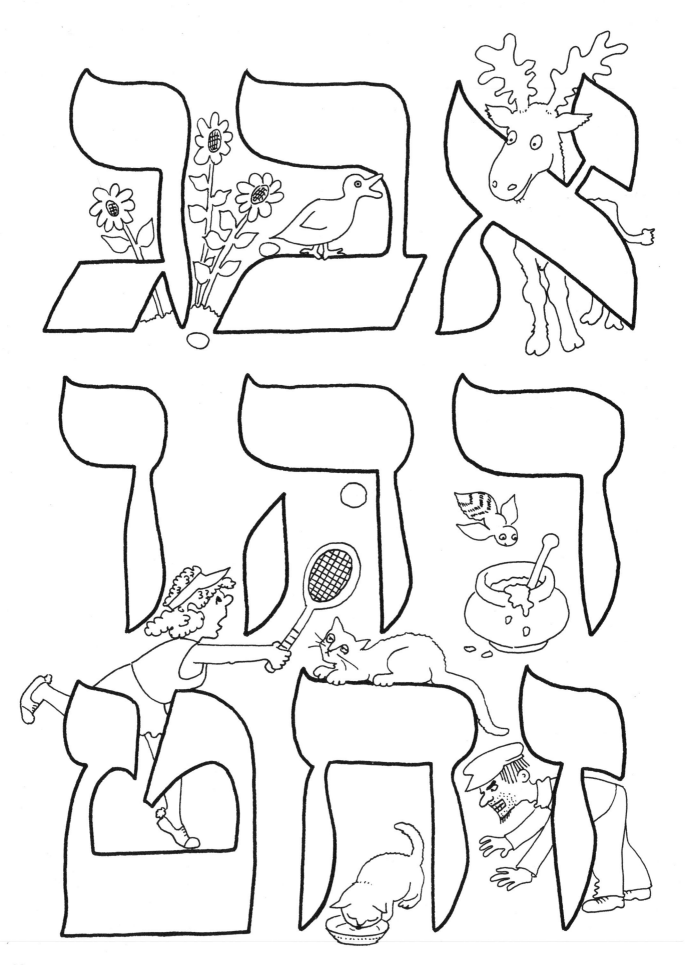